We're going to a
BIRTHDAY PARTY

Words by

Martha Mumford

Illustrated by

Cherie Zamazing

BLOOMSBURY
CHILDREN'S BOOKS
LONDON OXFORD NEW YORK NEW DELHI SYDNEY

We're going to a birthday party.
Come and join the fun!

Can you find the PARTY HATS?

Yes!

Run, run, run!

We're going to a birthday party.
Look, how sweet!

Watch out for the DUCKLINGS . . .

Quack!

Quack!

Cheep!

We're going to a birthday party.
Come and join the fun!
Can you find the red balloons?

NICE & CHEEP

Beautiful Balloons

Yes!

Run, run, run!

We're going to a birthday party.

Trot, trot, neigh!

Watch out for the HORSES . . .

Quick,
out of the way!

We're going to a birthday party.
Come and join the fun!
Can you find
the CANDLES?

Yes!

Run,
run,
run!

We're going to a birthday party.
Hello, friendly sheep!

Watch out for the
LITTLE LAMBS...

Baaa!

Baaa!

Leap!

We're going to a birthday party.
Come and join the fun!
Can you find the PARTY CAKE?

Yes! Run, run, run!

Specials
Carrot cake
Cupcakes
Bun-dt cake

Remember!
Special
surprise!

We're going to a birthday party.
Quick, through the park!

We're going to a birthday party.
Come and join the fun!
Can you find the PRESENTS?

Yes! Run, run, run!

Now we've gathered all we need,
it's time to celebrate.
COME ON! It's party time – don't be late!

Quick, quick,
little lambs –
baa, baa, leap!

Quick, quick, puppies –

woof, woof, bark!

Quick, quick, horses -

trot, trot, neigh!

Quick, quick, ducklings -

quack, quack, cheep!

Quick, quick, little buns - run, run, run!

Everyone, let's dance and sing –
now it's time to play!
Light the candles, cut the cake . . .

For Theodore, Giorgio and Gianna
- C.Z.

BLOOMSBURY CHILDREN'S BOOKS
Bloomsbury Publishing Plc
50 Bedford Square, London WC1B 3DP, UK
29 Earlsfort Terrace, Dublin 2, Ireland

BLOOMSBURY, BLOOMSBURY CHILDREN'S BOOKS and the Diana logo are trademarks of Bloomsbury Publishing Plc

First published in Great Britain in 2023 by Bloomsbury Publishing Plc

Text copyright © Bloomsbury Publishing Plc 2023
Illustrations by Cherie Zamazing, based on the original characters by Laura Hughes
Illustrations © Laura Hughes 2023

Cherie Zamazing has asserted her right under the Copyright, Designs and Patents Act, 1988, to be identified as Illustrator of this work

A catalogue record for this book is available from the British Library
ISBN HB: 978 1 5266 3222 7   ISBN PB: 978 1 5266 3223 4   ISBN eBook: 978 1 5266 3215 9
2 4 6 8 10 9 7 5 3 1

Printed and bound in China by Leo Paper Products, Heshan, Guangdong

MIX
Paper from
responsible sources
FSC
www.fsc.org   FSC® C020056

To find out more about our authors and books visit www.bloomsbury.com and sign up for our newsletters